If you've read *Jack and the Beanstalk*, skip this page.

If you haven't, read on ...

Once upon a time a mean giant stole a magic hen that laid golden eggs from Jack's family.

So Jack climbed up a beanstalk to Giant Land and got her back with the help of the giant's wife, Rose.

The giant chased after him and was half way down the beanstalk when Jack chopped it down.

That was the end of the giant.

But not of story ...

Chimps – very easy books for beginners
Large type
Short words
Short sentences
An illustration on every page
And fun!
With a twist in the tale!

This is the fifth **Chimp**
The other four are:
Cookie the Cat
Cookie and Curley
Flash Fox and Bono Bear
Two Mad Dogs

Derek Keilty

Illustrated by Terry Myler

THE CHILDREN'S PRESS

To Sarah-Jane and Rebekah,
with love

First published 2003 by
The Children's Press
an imprint of Anvil Books
45 Palmerston Road, Dublin 6

2 4 6 8 7 5 3 1

ISBN 1 901737 45 4

Typeset by Computertype Limited
Printed by Colour Books Limited

Contents

1 The Visitors

This is Jack.

And this was Jack's back garden after he had chopped down the beanstalk.

Now it's *full* of beanstalks.
Seven to be exact and all
growing very tall.

They grew from the handful
of beans Jack's mum had
tossed out of the window.

Missus Hanratty, who lived next door, hated them.

They cast a shadow over her garden where she liked to sunbathe. So she always had a stripy suntan.

'I'll *have* to do something about them,' she would say.

Missus Mudd, on the other side, loved them. She was into nature, which meant she was kind to trees and flowers and birds and animals.

'I'm glad you planted those bean trees,' she would say.

'Stalks. Bean*stalks*,' Jack would correct her.

Anyway, love them or hate them, the beanstalks grew taller and taller.

One night, when Jack and his mum were asleep, one of the beanstalks began to sway.

A giant foot appeared near the top. Then another. They wore the worst-looking fluffy slippers you ever saw.

Then someone gave a yelp.

'Sshhh! Be quiet, you big oaf!' another voice snarled.

'I slipped. It's this drippy beanstalk. I'm sure I've broken a toenail.'

'You and your toenail. Scat!'

Four giants – Fe, Fi, Fo and Fum – climbed down the beanstalks into Jack's garden.

'Fi and Fo, get the gold from the house,' said Fe. 'Fum, we'll grab the hen.'

'How come you boys always get the easy part?' whined Fi.

'Stop moaning and get on with it,' ordered Fe.

So Fi and Fo tip-toed over to the back of the house.

As they were far too big to get inside, they gawked through windows and poked fingers through doors.

When Fe and Fum opened the barn, the hen woke up from a lovely dream.

She had been dreaming she could fly as high as an eagle.

She was not a happy bird.

'Bok! Bok! Bok!' she clucked in rage, flapping her wings and filling the barn with feathers and straw.

'Silly ol' goose,' said Fum.

'That goose is a hen that lays golden eggs,' hissed Fe. 'Hurry up and catch her.'

'Will I give her a whack on the head?' asked Fum.

'You do no such thing or I'll murder you.'

Fum grabbed the hen and put her into a sack.

'Now what?' he asked.

'Now we scares 'em so they won't come after us.'

'Brill!' said Fum.

'Course it is! *I* thought of it! I'm one smart giant!'

Jack's mum opened one sleepy eye. Four faces stared in at her through the window. They were singing:

I'm Fe! I'm Fi!
  I'm Fo! I'm Fum!
We smell the blood
  Of a stupid mum.
If she's still here
  When we come back,
We'll grind her bones
  To make our snack!

'Ahhhhh,' screamed Jack's mum. She jumped out of bed and ran down to Jack's room.

'Spot on!' grinned Fe. 'Now, back up the beanstalks and sharpish!'

Jack woke with a start when his mum burst into his room yelling, 'There are giants outside my window. Lots!'

'Very odd,' said Jack. 'The giant went splat, remember?'

'There are more,' she cried. 'Come on, I'll show you.'

They hurried to her room.

But there were no giants. Only the full moon shining in.

'See? Nothing! It was just a nightmare. A silly old nightmare,' Jack told his mum.

2 The Beanstalks

The next morning Jack awoke to the sound of chopping.

He rushed outside to find his mum chopping down the beanstalks with a huge axe.

There was only one left.

'What's happening, Mum?'

'Burglary! The hen is gone. The gold is gone. It's those giants I saw at the window. But would you believe me?'

Missus Mudd was in tears.

'It's murder! That's what it is! Why did you do it?'

Jack's mum pointed to the empty barn. 'We've been burgled. By giants. They came down by beanstalk.'

Missus Mudd looked at her as if she'd gone bonkers.

'About time, too!' Missus Hanratty called from her window. 'But why did you have to do it so early? I'm losing my beauty sleep.'

'Well, don't get up today then,' snapped Missus Mudd. 'You sure need a lot of sleep.'

While they were all arguing, Jack went over to the last beanstalk and looked up.

Then he started to climb it.

'Where are you going?' shouted Mum.

He stopped halfway up and yelled, 'I'm going back up.'

'Come down at once! There
are four big giants up there.
They'll kill you.'

'They've stolen our hen and
our gold. We just can't let
them get away with it.'

'Take care,' moaned Mum.

'Not to worry. I'll be back
for supper.'

3 Giant Land

Jack soon reached the top and stepped off into Giant Land.

'Still as bare as ever,' he thought, gazing round at the grey rocky landscape.

A signpost read: *Castle half a kilometer. Giant Land welcomes careful drivers.*

When he arrived at the castle, he sneaked round to the back and peered in.

The four giants – Fe, Fi, Fo and Fum – were sitting round the great table in the kitchen.

They were a grisly bunch.

Fe was the brains of the outfit. When he added 2 and 2, he nearly always got 4.

Fi wasn't quite as sharp. He signed his name with an X as he couldn't write.

Fo was even thicker. He couldn't read.

Fum was the hit man. He was pretty handy with a club. When he made contact, that is.

Luckily for his hit record, most people fled when they saw him coming.

'Ha! You should have seen the old girl's face. We gave her a real scare,' purred Fe.

'We got the hen back,' said Fi. 'Now we're rich again.'

'Pa would have been proud of us,' sighed Fo.

Suddenly Jack felt a huge hand grab him.

'Gotcha!' growled Fum.

He dragged Jack inside.

'Look who I found snooping about outside.'

'Nice of you to drop in.'

Fe gave him an evil smile. 'You must be the famous Jack. Our poor late Pa told us all about you. Murderer! Thief!'

'*You're* the thieves – the lot of you!' shouted Jack. 'You won't get away with this.'

They all fell about laughing.

'So what are you going to do about it?' sneered Fe.

So Fum threw Jack into a black hole of a dungeon and slammed the door.

'Great, just great!' thought Jack as he looked around.

4 Prisoner!

The dungeon was dark and damp, with only one tiny window high up in the wall.

Jack leaned against the door and sighed.

'Gets cold at night,' said the voice of an old woman. 'You can have one of my scarves.'

Jack squinted through the darkness and saw a shadow sitting under the window.

'Who are you?' Jack asked.

The old woman gawked at him. 'My word! It's you, isn't it? Young Jack?'

Jack stared back.

'You're Rose, the giant's wife! The nice one who saved me. But what are you doing here – in the dungeon?'

'I've been stuck here ever since they found out I helped you to get away.

'I knew you'd grow up to be a fine lad, not like them morons of stepsons of mine.'

'That's terrible,' said Jack.
'But how are we going to get
out of here?'

'Can't be done!' sighed Rose.
'I did have a plan once, years
ago, but it didn't work. So I
started knitting to pass the
time. Scarves mostly. Short
ones, long ones…'

Jack picked up one. 'This one must be a mile long...but why is the wool so strong? It's more like string.'

'That's the kind of wool they have up here.'

'Gives me an idea,' said Jack. 'Pity they didn't put us into a tower with a window...'

5 Panic Stations

Jack's mum and Missus
Mudd were getting sore necks
from looking up the beanstalk.

They hadn't moved all day or
even had lunch.

Then, out of the blue,
Missus Mudd said, 'I'm going
to climb up there, too!'

Jack's mum almost fainted.
'You can't be serious. You're
not wearing proper boots.'

'Sod the boots. I've got to
find out what's going on.'

'I think you're very brave.'
Missus Mudd was quite a
good climber and soon she
was almost at the top.

Jack's mum, nerves on end,
hurried into the house.

'Oh, I must have a cup of
tea,' she gasped.

By an amazing chance, Missus Hanratty peered over the fence just then. Seeing the garden empty and the axe propped against the last beanstalk, she had a great idea.

'Hmm, since they're all up in the sky,' she muttered, 'they can STAY up there!'

She shot over the fence, lifted the axe and chopped down the last beanstalk.

Missus Mudd had just got off the beanstalk when she saw it topple over and vanish.

'That's torn it! How am I to get back?'

Back on earth, Jack's mum came back out of the house.

'Oh, poor Jack!' she cried, when she saw the fallen beanstalk. 'This is terrible! I'll never see you again.'

She went into a panic. She picked up the phone and dialled the first number that came into her head.

It was the fire brigade.

6 Mudd to the Rescue

In the dungeon in Giant
Land, Jack and Rose sat
knitting.

'I'll never get the hang of
this,' Jack said as he dropped
another stitch. 'And I *still*
can't think of an escape plan.'

'Me neither. In three years!'

All of a sudden, they heard
footsteps just outside the door.

'Pssst!' said a voice.

'Missus Mudd!' cried Jack.
'Fancy being rescued by you!'

'Hang on! You're not
rescued yet! And I don't see
how we're going to escape.
The beanstalk has gone!'

Jack looked stunned, then he leapt to his feet. 'I've got a plan. If only we could get out of this place. Can you open the door from the outside?'

'I don't think so,' Missus Mudd called back. 'It's far too strong for me to break down.'

Then her voice changed,
'Well, of all the luck...'
'What is it?' Jack broke in.
'The key is in the lock!'

And so it was. Fum had left
it there last time he threw in
some gruel and stale bread.

As Missus Mudd opened the door, Jack stuffed the very long string scarf that Rose had knitted into his bag.

He shouted to her, 'Come on!'

Rose stared at him.

'I'm not going to leave you here. You'll come back with us. But first we must get our hen and the bags of gold.'

In the castle kitchen, the giants had fallen asleep after an extra large lunch.

Jack quietly dragged the two sacks of gold outside while Missus Mudd carefully put the hen into a sack.

Fum opened a big sleepy eye, waved a giant fist and yawned. 'Don't think I could manage another bite.'

Then he fell asleep again.

'Let's scarper,' whispered Jack as they crept outside.

They hurried along the road to the entrance to Giant Land but they had only got half way there when they heard a rumble and a roar.

'Sounds like the giants waking up,' panted Jack.

'Let's step on it,' gasped Missus Mudd.

7 Back to Earth

Down in Jack's garden, the fire chief shook his head.

'Sorry, Missus, but all the ladders I have, put end to end, couldn't reach that high.'

'Poor Jack,' sobbed Jack's mum. 'I wish I'd never set eyes on those silly beans. I'll never eat beans on toast again.'

Suddenly
something
began falling from
the sky.

Something very
very long.

It looked like
a ladder.

Everyone stared
as it fell.

It didn't quite reach
the ground.

It ended level
with the roof
of Jack's
house.

A moment later, three
figures were seen scrambling
down through the clouds.

'It's Jack!' cried his mum.

HELP!
THEY ARE AFTER US!

Jack was shouting at them
but it was only when he was
halfway down that they could
hear what he was saying.

'Help! They're after us!'

Jack's mum called to the fire chief. 'Forget the ladders. Get that black thingummy.'

The firemen spread open the blanket underneath the ladder, then shouted, 'Jump!'

Missus Mudd jumped first, followed by Rose. The weight of the two bags of gold they were carrying made them so heavy that they almost ripped through the blanket.

Then Jack dropped the
hen who, for one split second,
thought she could fly!

Jack tied the end of the
string ladder around his wrist
and jumped.

'Quick, we have to unravel
the ladder before the giants
get to the top.'

8 In the End

When the giants woke up
and found their prisoners –
and the hen – had gone, they
set out in hot pursuit.

But they took a wrong turn
and didn't get to the spot
where Jack had fixed the top
of the ladder until the others
were halfway down.

Fum was the first to reach the ladder but as he began to climb down, he said, 'This doesn't feel very safe!'

'You're always moaning,' shouted Fe. 'Get a move on! We've all got to get down!'

'There's got to be a quicker way of doing this,' said Jack.

Then he caught sight of the hose reel on the side of the fire engine. 'Bingo!'

He tied the string to the hose and began turning the reel.

It worked! The ladder unravelled ten times as fast.

Fum noticed what was happening and screamed, 'Back up the ladder or we'll end up like poor Pa.'

They began to scramble back up as hard as they could.

As they did, the ladder became shorter and shorter.

It finally ran out just as the last giant set foot in Giant Land.

'Hurraaay!' everyone on the ground cheered.

Jack's mum brought them all inside for tea. 'I never want to see another beanstalk – or a bean – as long as I live.'

'If I'd known what was up there, I'd have chopped those beanstalks down myself,' said Missus Mudd.

On the way back to Giant
Castle, Fe was in a rage.

'It's your fault,' he said to
Fo. 'You took the wrong road.
Didn't you see the signpost?'

'It's not my fault,' wept Fo.
'I can't read.'

'That hen,' said Fe, 'we
gotta get her back. I have a
plan. Make a note, Fi.'

'I can't write,' sobbed Fi.

'What a bunch!' snarled Fe.

In a few days things began to get back to normal.

Missus Mudd gave half the gold that Jack had given her to the earth society.

Rose bought a lovely little cottage near the sea.

Missus Hanratty never did own up to chopping down the last beanstalk but Jack's mum said she was Suspect Number One.

As for the garden, Jack realised that the only way his mum would get a good night's sleep was if he covered the entire garden with a patio.

So he did!

This is **Derek Keilty's** first book for children. You can, however, read more stories written and illustrated by him on his interactive kids website at *www.keilty.btinternet.co.uk*.

Derek lives with his wife, twin daughters and a rabbit beside a beautiful mountain in Belfast and enjoys nothing better than sitting with a notebook scribbling down new stories.

Terry Myler has illustrated all the **Chimp** books. In addition, she has illustrated all the **Elephant** series (books to read if you're slightly older).

If you want to learn to draw yourself, have a look at her book *Drawing Made Easy*